winner
michigan writers cooperative press
2020 fiction contest

BLUETONGUE
and Other Michigan Stories

Ryan Shek

Michigan Writers Cooperative Press
P. O. Box 2355
Traverse City, Michigan 49685

ISBN-13: 978-1-950744-04-6

Book cover by Amy Hansen
Book interior by Daniel Stewart

Contents

Ed's Baby 1
Bluetongue 13
Still Living 26
Histories My Brothers Taught Me 40

Acknowledgements 45
About the Judge 46
About the Author 47
About Michigan Writers Cooperative Press 48
Other titles available from Michigan Writers Cooperative Press 49

BLUETONGUE
and Other Michigan Stories

Ed's Baby

Ed Hayes calls and says somebody vandalized his cow last night. I mean to ask just what in the hell he means, but Ed blurts out, "They painted a face on her."

I stand in my kitchen and try to picture it, but it's early, six in the morning, and the potatoes haven't even cooked through. Ed Hayes is hot wax dripping out of my phone and I hold the receiver away from my head, rub the sleep from my eyes. I tell him to sit tight and I hang up, slide a frying pan, half-cooked eggs, into the fridge. Ed Hayes didn't say so, but I know he's been waiting up for me. I fight on my boots, drive over.

"Can you believe it?" Ed asks.

We're standing at the edge of his pasture and I listen to the click-click of the electric fence, the plunger sounds the cattle make, hooves sinking into muck-snow and shit. "Where is she?"

"Her, next to the bull." Ed points to a large bull and a handful of heifers. Sure enough, there's Ed's Baby. A black and white dairy cow teetery as the day he bought her. There's a spot of orange across her hide and I can see the paint glistening in the morning, in the sun's sleepy, yellow beams. She looks like a canvas and wears a bright circle, two dotted eyes and a grin.

I lean on a post, careful not to touch the surging electric fence. "What do you make of it?"

"Make?" Ed spits the word out like a wad of chew. "I don't make a goddamn thing. Scratch that. I'll make sure it don't happen again."

Ed starts toward the barn, a two-story so old its paint flakes off in butterfly-sized chips, and motions for me to follow.

"What do I have you doing today?" he asks.

I shrug. I have the burst pipe to fix and the chuck to get to. At home, I've got my clothes to pack, my things to box up. A new job to worry about.

"I've got the chuck," I say.

"That can wait."

Ed stands before the barn and waits for me to see it. It doesn't take long. A big smiley face gleams across the double doors. Orange and bright like a road sign. A silly looking thing with two great big ears and no teeth, like a child's coloring book.

"This one showed up yesterday," Ed says. "That's three now."

"Where's the other?"

"Silo."

Ed holds the barn door open and I duck inside. It's cold, too cold to smell anything except the stinging fresh air. I clap my hands together, blow into them. The barn doesn't have stairs, just a ladder leading up to the hay loft. It's the first time I've seen Ed climb it and he's having trouble getting over the ledge, so I hold my arms out above my head, under his butt, just in case. He pulls himself up and pokes his head out, looks down at me.

"Did you get my letter?" Ed asks.

"What letter?"

"Must've gotten lost. 'Get your ass up here,' it said."

I smile and climb the ladder and see what all this business is about. Ed's got a lantern and a big deer shine up there, a couple chairs propped near the hay door. The door overlooks the pastures and peering through it, I feel like I'm standing in a sniper's nest. Ed sits down, points to a cooler. "You eat any of that stuff?"

I open the lid: dried venison, melon, and a couple good-sized peaches. I pick out a peach, look out the hay door. From up here I can see just about everything: the cows striding through the pasture, the outbuildings, the long driveway, the forest line way out back. Almost half the farm.

"Take the afternoon off and come back at nine," Ed says. "We're going to camp out and catch this joker."

Ed's Baby is a Canner Cutter, which means Ed bought her crippled off the meat market. A Hereford bull caught her in the eye with his horn and popped it clear out, led to a nasty infection. When Ed first brought her stumbling into the pasture, it looked like someone pumped her empty socket full of cottage cheese and rubber cement. I'd been working for Ed two weeks, but he put me in charge of her life. "Don't let her die," he said, like I had a say in what happened. To me, she looked like a goner, like any dying, dried up cull cow they sell at the beef auction.

At the house, I start packing again. Clothes and movies and pots and pans, things I need and things I need to throw away. I box everything up, move my things into the living room. I'm running back and forth, all through the house, sliding boxes over the hardwood, when my phone buzzes on the countertop. I check and see two messages. The HR people in Grand Rapids want to know if I'm settled in—if I know my new schedule. The second message is from Ed Hayes. He tells me to find my shotgun and whatever shells I have lying around. Bring them to the farm, he says.

"You could use my .22." Ed pauses like he's expecting me to pick up. "But that won't do much good if things got ugly. Not exactly a killer is it?"

Ed Hayes trails off and the message ends. I call him back, but he doesn't answer.

I'll have to talk some sense into him. Shooting a vandal isn't a very reasonable thing to do, and of course, I'm not willing to do it. Ed must think an armed militia is out spray-painting his farm, but it's probably a couple kids. Probably somebody we know.

"Where's your 12 gauge?" Ed asks. He's standing on the concrete steps to his house, wearing long underwear and a pair of Carhartt bibs. He pushes a fuzzy poof-ball hat further up his forehead and stirs a cup of coffee.

"At the house," I say. "Where's your coat?"

"Coat, moat, boat, don't you worry about me." Ed disappears into the house and comes back out with a jacket on, another cup of coffee, a .30-06 on one shoulder, the .22 on his other. "Here."

Ed hands me a cup of coffee and sticks out the .22. I wave it off and he cocks his head at me, confused and on-guard like I swore at him in French or something.

"I don't think I'll be needing that."

"Need? You'll take it. No telling what people might do."

I take the gun, realize now's not the time to press him. Ed adjusts the rifle on his shoulder and starts down the driveway, sips his coffee in the dark. "We should get a couple rounds in, circle the fence a few times. Check for tracks before we wait out in the barn."

"Okay," I say. "But what about the warehouse and the fruit stand and the slaughterhouse too?"

"Don't worry, we'll check those." Ed takes long steps into the snow, turns back toward me. "When do you leave?"

"Two days."

He almost stops.

"They think I've already moved."

People in town call Ed's Baby EB for short. Ed likes to show her off to all the other beef farmers in the county, the few who are left. EB is a novelty. Not only did she survive the eye infection, but she gave birth to three healthy heifers, one right after another. Ed says EB saved his herd, but that's just a story he likes to tell. Truth is, Ed's herd is nothing like it used to be. Fifty to sixty head, half of what it was three years ago, when I started working for him.

EB keeps the conversations away.

She gives Ed a way out of questions he's not ready to answer. Questions about his age or his health, how much it would cost to rent the pastures. The big-timers want to know if Ed's ready to sell the farm, but he responds all the same. He dresses the EB story up real nice and works all the right angles. A left-for-dead cow that shits gold. People around here think EB is the cattle farming wonder of the world and that Ed is some kind of sage, the kind of mogul that'll survive this industry. Of course, he isn't. Not even now. Not even in our little corner of Allegan County.

Ed and I sip the rest of our coffee and hang our cups upside down on the pasture posts, the thin metal ones that support the electric fence.

"What're they starting you at?" It's not the first time he's asked me.

"$19.50."

Ed goes quiet and I know he's trying to work out the math in his head.

"Remember," I tell him. "It's about the benefits. I get health insurance and retirement and dental too."

Ed starts walking again, talks over his shoulder. "I can't compete with that."

I want to tell him I know, or that I'm sorry, or that if things were different, maybe I'd stay. But that would be another lie. "Really, Ed. Thanks for keeping me around, for teaching me how to do all this stuff."

"Hell," Ed says. "It wasn't easy. You aren't the sharpest shit."

We round the corner post and watch the herd gather near the barn, under the barn lamps. The wind is picking up and the snow's drifting bad, but all those bulls and heifers look warm huddled together. Steam rises up off their bodies and catches the light like a hundred of those old-time trains—the coal engines Butch Cassidy and his wild bandits robbed. The cows look like a cozy group of them firing their engines, rolling out the station real slow.

"Look there."

Ed holds out his arm and points to the slaughterhouse. The building is old, brick built. It looks like a deep, dark square from where we're standing—two football fields away. A teensy tiny light catches one of the window panes. It's just a tiny bright spot. A sharp, distant glare.

"Did you leave a lamp on?"

Ed stares for a good long while, adjusts his rifle.

"Not a chance," he says.

A teenager shot Ed's son over something small, a drug deal gone wrong or something. They had a closed casket funeral and Ed will still grouse about the morticians. He'll say, "Eight thousand dollars to bury my boy and no one got to see how sharp he looked." For good reason. Ed's boy was shot in the face. The day he told me, Ed pressed a finger to his cheek—just below the eye—pressed until the blood flushed out of his flesh and left a little white ring on his skin. "Right here," he said. "The expert-doctor said the bullet severed Brandon's brain stem. He died before you even made it out of diapers."

Ed points to the slaughterhouse, to the big, rusty door.

"I want you over there."

The light glares through the windows, but when I look in, I can't see anyone. Just the gleam of the lamp. It reflects off the processing table and lights up the hooks and pulleys that hang from the rafters. Pointed and menacing, spooky silhouettes.

"If they were smart, they'd have propped this door open." Ed shucks the .30-06 off his shoulder and tries the slaughterhouse door. Locked.

I can't see his face, but I know Ed's serious by the sound of his voice. He sounds too focused, too drill sergeant, for this to be a stupid, confused teenager—a neighborhood-kid spray-painting for kicks.

"Ed." His name feels like a brick in my stomach. It's heavy and hard to pull out. "We should take it easy."

"Wait here," Ed says. "I'm going round back."

Before I can do anything, Ed zags around the corner and leaves me standing there, gripping the .22 and guarding the big, rusty door. I wait, listen to the wind, to the crunch-crunch of Ed's footsteps. He's moving soft and slow through the snow like a buck sauntering up to a salt lick.

Thud-clank and the back door opens. Ed goes stomping in.

As I understand it, Brandon Hayes didn't enjoy cattle farming, but Brandon Hayes would've enjoyed EB. He had a soft spot for anything hurt or sorry, whatever couldn't take care of itself, Ed says.

One winter, before Brandon was shot, before Brandon was even old enough to read, Ed's wife got sick. I don't remember what she came down with, but Ed said she ran cold, real cold, was unable to talk and could hardly move. Back then, the farmhouse was one shit place, had ply-board windows and paper-thin walls. Ed killed himself keeping the wood stove going, could hardly do it all on his own. Brandon helped even though he was just a small fry. He slipped on his mittens and marched to the woodpile, fetched his logs one or two at a time, as many as his little arms could carry.

"He had a rough go, but we all have our troubles," Ed said. "Even this calf."

EB had just given birth to her first calf, but the calf wouldn't latch out in the pastures. To keep her from starving, Ed moved her into the barn, into her own little stall, and had me prepare a bottle.

"People like to throw things away when times get tough, but just lookit EB."

I gave Ed the bottle, watched the calf resting her head in Ed's lap. Her eyelids opened and shut; her coat was still wet from the womb. She chewed at Ed's finger until she took the bottle and gulped down the milk.

"Can you believe those farmers just threw old girl away?"

I shook my head.

"You think that's right? To just throw things away?"

I didn't say anything. Ed stared up at me.

"It's never okay to throw away somebody who needs you," he said.

The graffiti on Ed's slaughterhouse wall looks like all the rest: a bright orange face, except this one is the biggest face yet. It spans maybe six feet, a man's wingspan across, like someone stood on tip-toe to paint it. Inside the circle, two sloppy ovals stare out like orange olives, and the mouth curves up in a goofy, crude grin.

"They must've just left," Ed says. He locks the slaughterhouse door behind me and hoists himself up on the processing table. He pushes the ground chuck and butcher's paper across the shiny metal, which leaves little streaks of blood.

"Got to hand it to them. It's kind of a funny picture." Ed is smiling back at the face like he was watching his favorite TV show, like he was eating chips on the sofa. "What do you think?"

I walk up to the face, brush my fingers across its mouth. "I think whoever did it must be gone."

"Why's that?" Ed grunts.

"Paint's dry and the slaughterhouse doesn't smell like aerosol."

Ed tilts his head, sniffs the air and scoots off the table. "Here." He fishes a flashlight from his bibs pocket and holds it out for me, leads me outside. The snow is coming down heavy and blows around in long drifts. My flashlight illuminates the big fat falling flakes like hundreds of floating constellations.

"Here we go," Ed says.

He shines his light down on a trail of boot prints—a faded path that snakes out to the pastures, the opposite direction of where we came. The trail's been snowed on, blown around. It looks faded, hours old.

"Let's go," Ed says.

I accepted the Grand Rapids job the second they offered. Plastic manufacturer up in the Kentwood area. My cousin mentioned open interviews and I took the day off, told Ed I was visiting a college counselor up at Grand Valley, was fixing to enroll. A job's a job, but education—that's doing something. That's bettering yourself.

My plan was to feel the place out, but on the drive, I decided to leave. I was tired of the good-old-days stories and the death of the American farmer, tired of hearing about EB.

Ed takes long steps through the snow, long careful-not-to-fall steps. I shine my light down at his tracks and then the vandal's, back and forth between both sets of prints like a cop. I notice how similar they are. The gait, the distance between feet. The depth. Ahead of me, Ed kicks up big white puffballs of snow that get blown away by the wind, into my face. I turn my back, look down at my own trail. It looks different, but sort of the same. It's hard to tell.

"Looks like he was heading to the barn," Ed yells. He stops at the driveway and waits up for me. "Every day this week. Same face, somewhere new."

"You should call the police," I tell him.

"What're they going to do?" Ed asks. "They have real things to look after, not silly shit like this."

"You'll have to do something."

"You're right about that," Ed says. "I'm going to have to hire two people now. One to work and one to look after the place."

I shrug, let the comment sit there between us.

"Right—let's get to it," Ed says.

I think the Grand Valley lie bothered Ed more than anything. That whole drive back from Grand Rapids, I thought about what I'd tell him. He doesn't have children to run the farm, but the job was too good to pass up, would change my life for the better. Best-case scenario, he'd say I was making the right call. Worst case, he'd fire me for the hell of it. Turns out, he didn't say anything. He just listened as I rambled about college, about stumbling into some job fair, about getting offered the position on the spot. I told him how unexpected it all was and that part was true for Ed, an old man left to run a failing beef operation—no warning, no hint.

"I'll figure something out" is all he would say.

The trail cuts through the driveway and wraps around the warehouse, for hundreds of yards, with no direction or sense. It looks like the meter reader had trouble finding the electric box, like the cable guy followed some endless, underground cord.

"Joker took his legs for a joyride," Ed says.

Ed shines his light up the trail. It stops at the barn's side door. "Check it out."

He follows the trail up to the barn, but doesn't brief me with a single word. Not "watch out" or "be careful" or even "hey, what if?" He leans his rifle against the wall, pulls the door along its track and holds it open for me. I squeeze in. It's dark inside and I find myself standing in a big barn stall with a dozen head of cattle. I can't see them, but I can hear them breathe—whoosh in, whoosh out—a chorus of deep, cavernous breaths.

Ed squeezes through the doorway without his rifle, walks through the shit and straw, searches for the light switch. He flicks it on and I see what I've been smelling. There's more than a dozen cows pinned in there with us. They stand in still pools of their own piss and are each painted with bright orange faces. Their backs and their bellies, their white and black hides. All together, they look like a Dr. Seuss storybook, a hokey art exhibit, a scene from the Allegan County Fair.

"Jesus," I say.

Ed puts his hands in his pockets and watches the cows. He kneels, looks underneath their sagging bellies, stares to the back of the herd.

The night EB gave birth to her first calf, Ed wanted me to stay up and bottle-feed her. He offered me overtime, double-time, the big bucks to stay. I agreed because I needed the money, but instead of heading in and getting his rest, Ed camped out with me. Not to work or to help or to make sure I was doing it right, but to talk about Brandon. He told me about his boy in the sandbox, his boy on the gridiron, his boy's first girlfriend and all the goofy things his boy did as a kid. I listened, but offered to head home after a while. It had gotten so late, I could tell he'd be out there all night.

"What," Ed said. "You got somewhere to be?"

"No," I said. "Just don't want you wasting your money is all."

Ed scoffed. "Don't worry about me."

Ed stands in the barn and looks at the cows. Their heads bob up and down, swing from side to side. Black eyes searching for feed. Ed doesn't move a muscle. He doesn't look at me; he doesn't look for a vandal. He watches all those stupid, bright faces. Those smiling, toothless grins.

"Ed, you do this?"

He doesn't answer, just walks toward his herd. As he gets close, half the cows turn east, the others turn west. One cow, in the back, stands still. The others jitter and part like a sea.

"Ed?"

Ed takes off his gloves and runs a bare hand over the cow's head. Under the barn light, I see the rutts of his face, the twist of a frown. Grief. He glances up.

"Wouldn't that be something."

Ed pets the cow and I can tell it's EB by the way she lets him brush her. She's blind and gentle and doesn't jerk or take a single step back. She lets Ed run his palm down her neck and across her hide, over her shoulders, back to the base of her throat.

"Easy, old girl." Ed whispers like I'm not there. "Looks like it's just you and me."

Bluetongue

On the fifth day, that's when my wife stroked out. It was after Trammell's boy bagged his first buck. I remember because of the bluetongue and because Trammell's boy couldn't keep his liquor down. It was his first time drinking and me and Johnny poured him whisky after whisky until he keeled over in the bushes, blue-faced and empty bellied, the pot of stew he'd sucked down smelling like vinegar and what else I couldn't tell you.

—Hold his hair back!

—Don't fall asleep.

We hollered at Trammell's boy as he crawled to the cabin, a purple stain soaking down his shirt as if Johnny had knifed his throat. He tried standing in the driveway and again at the door, but we were there to push him down, to fold him over and laugh. Trammell didn't find it funny. Heading in from the forest, he saw us hovering over his boy and barked up into our chests.

—Pick on someone your own damn size, Trammell said. He's sixteen!

—Easy, Tram.

Trammell shot up in Johnny's face and cocked a fist back like he'd run him through the belly with it. I hadn't seen Johnny fight anyone since he broke that tweaker's mouth out in Pullman and spent two and a half years writing prison letters to his old lady. Of course, that was young Johnny. The Johnny without plates in his back, or screws in his ankle, or teeth hanging off his gums like water-starved plants.

—You don't want me picking on you, Johnny said.

—Try me, big fuck.

Later at the cabin, after we smoked a little dope, Johnny twisted Trammell's arm around his back until I heard it crack. Crunch, like the sound of cinder block breaking open over concrete. Trammell yipped and fell to the porch and just sat there, still and stunned, looking around at all the trees.

—Is it broke?

Trammell's eyes rolled over Johnny and then wandered over me. He was trying to piece it all together.

—I don't know.

It was, but we didn't know that then. We helped him up. We stretched his forearm and bicep in all different directions. We kneaded his muscles with our hands, pulled at the ends of his fingers for good measure. Trammel moaned. I pinned my thumb against his wrist and felt for a pulse. I couldn't tell his heartbeat from mine. Johnny's dope hit me good and our hearts raced together, felt like bubbles gurgling out of an underwater chest.

—*Goddamn,* I said. I think you'll live.

I never married my wife.

I proposed once as a formality, but Ashley didn't know how to take me kneeling there in our living room, on the dog-shit carpet, the ceiling sagging over my head like that's where giants rested their feet. I didn't have a ring, but promised her one as part of the deal. I was serious about getting married.

—You ain't going to marry me, she said.

I got up off my knee and sat at the edge of our couch. Bananas, our cat, brushed against my leg. I reached down and pet the back of his neck.

—I'm trying to. What else are we going to do?

She shrugged. Rain pattered against the tin of our trailer, sounded romantic. I wanted to ask before the hunting trip, something about the distance—about being away for a while. It seemed as good a time as any.

—You think I want to get stuck here? she asked.

Bananas hopped atop the television set and sniffed an ashtray I'd left up there. He pawed it, walked between the rabbit ears. There was a long silence between me and Ashley. After a while, she put her feet in my lap for me to rub and I kneaded away at her skin. Her head hung back and rolled to the side, looking beautiful. I wished I had more hands, more fingers to comb through her hair, to scratch at her scalp and rub down her shoulders. I was feeling that way, hungry-handed, when she suddenly looked up at me.

—We're not *doing that*, she said.

Marriage killed Johnny.

Johnny's old lady killed Johnny.

Not figuratively, literally. Johnny and Patricia had some atom-bomb fight when we got back from the hunting trip, when he dropped me off to tend to Ashley and then rolled up into his driveway seven sheets to the wind. Whole thing started over groceries. Man ends up dead and his wife goes to prison because there wasn't a bag of chips to snack on or a can of soup to warm up.

Prosecutors said Patricia severed Johnny's vena cava, nicked his aorta. Doctors called it a sucking wound—no blood came out. It all slurped back up into his chest like a coolant leak and that must've been confusing for them both. Apparently, Johnny had something like thirty seconds to live, and if he knew it, maybe he would've gotten up off the couch, or apologized for being so rotten. Maybe, he would have said go to hell. Instead, Johnny just sat in front of his television, muttered, "Can't believe you actually got me." He was watching *M*A*S*H*.

Sometimes I picture it.

Hawkeye and Radar bump around a green army tent, do some television-doctor stuff. The TV light discoes over Johnny and Patricia and the sofa they're sitting on. Patricia stands there, stupid, as Johnny stops breathing, as everything distills in her brain. The laugh track crashes through the trailer like broken plates. Radar says, you got guts sir, you got guts.

The prosecutors say Patricia cleaned the knife and put it back on the kitchen counter. Then she took a shower and called the police. I heard the call in court.

—My husband, he's not breathing. He got in a fight with a guy and you should hurry. I don't think he's breathing.

The Saint Joe attorney wanted me to testify as a kind of character witness for the defense. To talk about Johnny and the terrible things I'd seen him do. It's not *ratting*, the attorney told me, you just sit before the court and tell them what you've seen.

I'd seen Johnny whip his old lady around their trailer like she was made of aluminum cans. I'd seen him pin her head against the wall and hiss in her ear. Thing is, I'd never seen any of that sober. Ashley and I would score dope at Johnny's house; it wasn't the kind of place to hang around in, or relax, or enjoy the game. And I wasn't stupid. I knew how those court things went. They get you up there looking nice before a jury and then all the sudden it's your name getting dragged through the muck. Like you were the bad guy. Like you were the one who got fed up with Johnny's horseshit and ended the whole thing.

On the hunting trip, Trammell's boy didn't know what to make of the bluetongue.

It's a disease. A deer disease and a nasty deer disease at that. A deer with bluetongue bleeds. Not outwardly, but inwardly—like how Johnny died. The heart and liver and kidneys and every other goopy thing starts pumping blood into the deer's body. It gets hot.

It feels like a tire fire taking off deep inside their bellies. And that's where you'll find them, near water.

I'd heard of hunters stumbling across whole graveyards of deer. Ten or twenty lying along riverbeds and creeks, bobbing by the dozens in little inland lakes. Eventually, I'd see it too—on the same hunting trip that started this whole mess, but first it was Trammell's boy, the buck he shot. The buck's throat was bloated and swollen and his tongue hung out of his face two sizes too big. To be sure about the bluetongue, I needed to know how Trammell's boy killed the buck.

—I don't think he noticed me at all, Trammell's boy said. He came right up, not scared or anything.

Johnny ran a skinning knife over the buck's ribs.

—Skinny feller.

—So what?

—Got bluetongue.

—We'll keep the rack at least, said Trammell.

—Now why would you go do that for?

—It's the boy's first buck.

—You think that's a trophy? Could've killed him with a hammer.

—What do you think? You want to take him home?

Trammell's boy shook his head. The buck was winched up high in a tree. We were about to take him down, to abandon the diseased carcass, but Johnny sank his knife deep into the buck's belly. He brought the blade down slow and steady as if he were unzipping a lady's pants. Everybody watched the hide, expecting a mess of worms or a swarm of bees to fly out, but there was nothing. Besides there being hardly any meat, the insides seemed normal. Not fetid or anything. Still not a good idea to eat anything diseased.

—Enough for breakfast, Johnny said.

It took a year or so for the trial to begin. Ashley had just gotten out of physical rehab and I loved having her back. To show her, I'd heat up TV dinners or buy takeout, surprise her with flowers or something. Things were easy when Ashley could hardly move. But then she got her body back before her mind. She'd heat up the oven, forget it was on, then smoke out the whole house. Some nights, she'd order pizza and stand up the delivery men. She couldn't remember a thing, but still wanted to be independent, even move out. I convinced her it was too dangerous, that she'd hurt someone, probably herself.

Over time, I made sure to disconnect the propane whenever I left the house, but she got wise to the phone lines. She could tell a ringtone from dead silence and so I stopped unplugging it whenever I went out. As for court, I had to bring her. I was afraid of the bills she might rack up and the trouble she could get into sitting around the trailer by herself. Long story short, she was there when I told the jury about Johnny and his wife Patricia. When I told the world about who they really were.

Court is a funny place.

Everyone's arguing over what you say like everything you say is the truth. It's all baloney. The truth isn't even something you know. At best, it's something you can remember. And the jury is just amazed to be there, like they are fulfilling some call from on high. Like it's God's work they're doing. Johnny's jurors spent most of the trial watching Patricia. They tried to gauge her reaction to testimony they didn't even understand. Some people you can't trust just by looking at them.

I sat my wife down on the right side of the courtroom so her good ear pointed to the wall. She complained she wouldn't be able to hear the testimony, but I told her she had to be close to the bailiff in case they needed to verify anything I might've said. She asked, how can I? I can't even hear what you're saying. I said, that's just the way things are.

—Did Jonathan Drawlers ever threaten Patricia Drawlers with physical violence? the prosecutor asked.

—A few times, I said.

—On more than five occasions?

—Less than five, I'd say.

—Did he ever threaten to *kill* Mrs. Drawlers?

—Depends on what you mean by threaten.

—Well, Mr. Vandenberg, what's your definition?

That was a tricky question. A lot of what Johnny said to his wife could've been taken seriously or left alone altogether. I thought about it in terms of me and Ashley. Before her stroke, when she wasn't so easy going, just my breathing could set her off. And there'd been times when I pinned her wrists together over her head and smothered her face with my belly. Those nights when she said something I wasn't prepared for, when she was hateful, or didn't take me seriously, when "I could kill you" took us places "you liar" or "you bitch" just couldn't.

Then there were the times we'd play Monopoly. When we'd pass GO before we passed out. When I'd fuck up the die count just to land on her hotels. When I had Marvin Gardens and North Carolina and all she needed was to get back on her feet.

It's one of those catch twenty-two things. You don't mean what you say, and you can't really say what you mean. Those nights, I think I meant to tell Ashley that I was worth something. That maybe, she was too.

—A threat is, I guess, something you don't necessarily follow through with, but could, I said. Johnny didn't. I don't think I got to sit up here and tell you that.

—I'm sorry if this is hard for you, Mr. Vandenberg. I understand Mr. Drawlers was a friend.

—They both are.

—And we thank you for being here, but Mrs. Drawlers is on trial for murder. And it would help if you told the court whether or not . . .

—Objection. Leading.

—Sustained.

—Sorry, your honor, the prosecutor said. I'll go back to the original question: Did Jonathan Drawlers ever threaten to kill his wife?

—Yes, but he couldn't mean it, I said.

—How would you know if he *meant* it?

—Obviously he didn't kill her.

—But you couldn't have known his intentions, could you have?

—No.

—But you did hear the threats?

—That's right . . .

—On more than one, but less than five occasions?

—Yes.

—No further questions.

Johnny was cooking a cut of that bluetongue buck when the police called. I remember steam rising up off the pan like smoke from a bowl and I answered around the third ring. Plugging one ear, I listened to the officer, watched Johnny stick that meat with his fork, heard the words *condition* and *emergency* and *unknown*. I thanked the man—the officer—and Johnny held the meat in front of my face. It looked good enough to eat.

—What's up? he said.

—It's Ashley.

—She fuck off?

—She's in bad shape.

They took her to Bronson, in Kalamazoo, seven and a half hours away. Johnny offered to drive us from Ishpeming. Seven and a half hours from the Upper Peninsula to the Lower Peninsula. I'd driven to Nashville in less time than that.

—What'd she get into? he asked.

—They haven't said.

—She swig a bottle? She hate you? You fuck her sister or something?

I shook my head. As far as I knew, she wasn't depressed or on any of the heavy shit. The police didn't say she had a stroke. I just knew she wasn't picking up, and that's why I called in the first place. Every morning me and Trammel and Johnny walked out to the hunting blinds, I rang Ashley. Every evening we got back to the cabin, I rang Ashley. For five days, no answer. I just thought she was mad at me for going on a hunting trip in the first place, but after seeing the marsh, and all those dead deer, I had enough. I called the police and gave them permission to break my door down. They found Ashley sitting in a pile of her own piss and shit, a mess of cat hair covering her lap from all the times Bananas begged to be fed or paid attention to.

Johnny drove down 131 with the windows rolled down. He let the forty degree air whip his face, enjoyed the pressure; the cold air cleared his head. It just stung my skin.

—Pit stop, he said.

Johnny pulled into a Route 66 station, took out his pipe.

—Want some?

He blew thick white smoke up into the air and I watched it roll out the windows like a steam stack. I waved it off. A lumber semi drove by, then another. I felt sick from all the driving, from thinking about Ashley and the state of our sofa. I hadn't slept since the first night of the trip.

—How about some beer? Johnny asked.

There's always been something about Johnny. I don't know how to say it exactly, but you can see it in the way he carries on, the way he moves. He swung that thirty pack through the parking lot like he had all the answers, like nothing could ever bother him. In his truck, he bit the heads off each airplane shot while steering with one hand, slugging them down at every other mile marker. I looked at the booze in the backseat, at the empty liquor and beer bottles.

I thought maybe if I watched Johnny, if I really paid attention, I could learn something. Maybe, he could teach me a thing or two.

The defense attorney wore a dusty attic suit and dull loafers. Silver-gray hair and a long pineapple face, something like Charlie Rose. He delivered his closing statements to the jury and wasn't too keen on Johnny. I suppose that was his job. When somebody ends up dead, there's hell to pay. If you're lucky, it's just your attorney who collects.

—And you've heard testimony here today, the attorney said, that when Jonathan Drawlers returned home from his five-day hunting trip in Ishpeming, he was drunk and high on methamphetamine. You heard the testimony of Bryce Vandenberg, a friend who shared a thirty pack of beer and twelve—twelve!—two-ounce shots with Mr. Drawlers in the hours leading up to his death. You've also heard the testimony of three police officers who routinely responded to domestic violence calls at Mr. Drawler's address. And when Mr. Drawlers, a meth-addicted alcoholic with a known history of domestic violence, saw that his wife had neglected to purchase groceries the night of November 18, he lost it. We are here, ladies and gentlemen, because Jonathan Drawlers dragged Patricia Drawlers around by her hair and threatened to kill her in cold blood. Why? Because he didn't have any food. Ladies and gentlemen, we are here because Patricia Drawlers defended herself. We are here so an innocent woman can walk free.

It was a very fine speech. Was it the truth? Nothing close. Johnny was never a very good husband and he certainly was a violent piece of work, but there's something to say about that jury. They saw what I knew about Patricia.

It didn't come out in court, but she'd stabbed him before. She fucked up his fingers pretty bad once. I remember Johnny showed up at the job site one day with a hand wrapped in t-shirts. He showed me his pinky, a dead, useless thing. He told me he got into it bad with Patricia, arguing, calling names, etcetera., and then Patricia went away in the kitchen for a while. When she came back out, she was holding one of those kitchen knives, just like the one she used to kill him. Fucking stone cold, Johnny told me. When he reached for it, Patricia thrust the knife up into the webbing of Johnny's fingers, up into his palm. That was before the drugs fried him, when he was twenty and could work a whole day with half a hand. When he had more fight.

I don't know why Johnny shrugged Patricia off and I don't know why Patricia stuck around just to make good. Johnny's murder seemed like a sure-fire bet to me, but it wasn't so obvious to Johnny himself. He was too loose, too good times.

—She told me to keep pushing it, Johnny said. She told me she'd get me right here, right in the chest.

Ashley wasn't all there at the hospital. She never got to see me strung out and slurring at the nurses, which saved me some bull. But I sat with her the night Johnny was killed. When he dropped me off, sped away, and was never seen alive again. I sat with her the next few nights, even after the police called me in for questioning. I wouldn't leave Ashley's side so the detectives visited the hospital. I would only go as far as the hallway just outside Ashley's room.

Finally, when Ashley woke up and could tell me from the orderlies, I told her everything. About Johnny. About Patricia. About Trammell. She didn't seem to know who I was even talking about.

—Johnny Drawlers, I said. He went hunting with me and Trammell. He comes home off the road and his wife stabs him. I was just with him.

—Hunting trip? she asked.

—It's where I been. Where I was when this all happened.

Ashley's forehead scrunched in a triangle of wrinkles. Her brain went searching for a memory she didn't have. It didn't seem possible to me, what all she could forget.

—I would know if you went on a hunting trip, she said.

—It was raining the day I left. You don't remember?

Ashley shook her head. I told her about the trip and Trammell's boy, about that skinny buck. I told her about all the dead deer I saw down at the marsh. I told her about how rattled I got, how she wouldn't pick up the phone, how after I'd seen it, I called the police. It was all a premonition, an omen, I told her. She listened like I was somebody new, like she'd never heard a story her whole life.

—What did it look like?

It all went like this: A bad wind blew in from the east. I couldn't hear anything out at the blinds, just the scrunching leaves and the whoosh-whipping branches. The wind carried a scent, a whiff. At first, it smelled no different than a dead opossum, but the closer I got to the creek, the worse it smelled. I decided to follow the creek a while. It was hard walking. My boots picked up muck and grew heavy and it was still dark—the sun just a red-burnt ring above me. Under the rattling branches, I saw the doe.

She was sick and skinny, her life on empty. I watched her drink from the water and I watched her reflection in the creek. Her snout broke the surface of the water, sent little lily-pad ripples in all different directions. Up ahead of her, the creek opened into a marsh. I saw bodies there. Two or three dozen deer, some rotted, most freshly dead. A couple doe sank down deep to the marsh's muddy bottom, some floated out in little islands by themselves. A tussle of three or four bucks clogged the creek's mouth, their legs and antlers locked up like some kind of dam.

Another strong wind blew by and suddenly the smell was bursting in my nostrils, like the whole world squeezed up there to die. I gagged, hacked up a long tail of snot-spit.

The doe kept drinking.

Her neck bulged with each sip; her coat gleamed in waves. Her tongue was swollen rotten. She picked up each hoof and set it down gently, like the creek was a bed of broken glass, or a hot bath she wasn't quite used to.

Ashley interrupted my story.

She was concerned about the doe. She wanted to know if it could smell those rotting corpses. Even for an animal, it seemed like a bad place to go, to drink from. I told Ashley about the bluetongue, about the organs and the bleeding and the heat. Sometimes, a deer will look for water just to lie in, a place to cool off while they die. She asked me more and more questions and I imagined how nice it'd feel to marry her.

—Do you think she knew?

—Knew what?

—That she would die there? Ashley asked. Like all those others?

I didn't know how to answer. The deer go to whatever body of water is closest. I explained how the state of the water wouldn't matter. It could've been filled with a hundred deer. It could've been sludge.

—The deer don't know nothing, I said. That's bluetongue. They drink and go belly up.

Still Living

My brother Bird's .22 rifle is pointing at my face and I tell him to watch it. He smiles and moves the gun so it points out the window and I go back to breaking up the pills on the dashboard. When they're ready, I flash the light over the field and look for eyes.

It's late and I have to get up in the morning. I have a brief to finish for my friend, Dick Bellingham. Dick said he tried to avoid a deer when he crashed his truck into the high side of a ditch and fell into a coma so deep the doctors presumed consent to amputate both his legs. Dick thinks a settlement for waking up without legs will be worth millions. It won't be, not by a long shot. Malpractice isn't my strong suit. I mostly handle divorce and domestic violence. The kicker, if it's appropriate to call it that, is that I, the doctors, and everyone else in the world knows the deer story is bullshit. Dick tried killing himself.

"Bend this bill Deano," Bird says and hands me a dollar bill from the driver's seat.

I try to flatten the wadded up single, but find it too wrinkled, too flaccid to snort anything with. There's a crisp hundred in my pocket so I roll that up and snort the lines. When I'm through, I lean forward and lick the pill-dust up with my tongue, but it's not easy. The road is all hardpack and washout and the truck jostles from side to side.

"There," Bird says. He taps the brakes and I stub my face against the dash. "A doe."

I hook the light out the window and shine the field like a prison tower. The light illuminates frozen corn stalks and drifting flakes of snow. Near the tree line, a pair of eyes shine back at us.

"Got it," I say.

I hold the doe in the spotlight and Bird hoists himself out the window, real slow, resting his gun on the roof. I hear metal scratch on metal above me and just before the shots ring out, I let out a big fat breath. Bird fires. Three quick pops and the eyes drop down like elevator buttons. Bird has shot the doe square in the forehead and we laugh and talk over each other as she tries to stand. We think she's a goner, but she rises on rickety legs and follows my light back to a line of woods, stumbles away.

"Tough mother," Bird says.

The still living doe has got me thinking about Dick Bellingham and what I need to write in his brief. The legal principles. The facts. The meaning. Although the doctors *did* presume consent to amputate, it's obvious the crash with its "subsequent amputation and resultant effects" was ultimately Dick's own kind of suicidal liability. The best I can do is get the case in front of a jury. Maybe they'll see how pitiful Dick is and give him some money he doesn't deserve. Even then, it's a long shot. Pity only gets you so far. And of course there's the other side to worry about, potential charges. But at least Dick has cleaned up since the accident. The crash got him sober. It softened his hard head. It bounced his life so hard off rock bottom that his enemies and friends gave him a pass for all the bullshit he's ever done, every drunk call he's ever made, every dollar he's ever stole, and every poor sonofabitch he's ever ripped off.

Even Dick's longtime ex-wife, Angie, moved in after the accident. That was hard for me to believe because I handled their divorce and saw first-hand how ugly things had gotten between them. But they seem on good terms now, Dick and Angie.

"Some things surprise you," I say.

Bird and I are watching the tree line. It's starting to snow pretty heavy now. The doe is good and gone.

"That deer's got a story," Bird says. He's looking down the long tunnel of our headlights. "Watch her have grandkids."

"You kidding?" I say. "She's probably fucked in the head."

"One of the lucky ones," Bird says. "You got any dope?"

I haven't smoked dope since the last time Bird stopped by the farm.

"Gave it up," I say. "Made me feel too accomplished."

"Bullshit."

I point to Bird's head. "Your work receptors, you know, up there in your brain, they light up like Christmas whenever you smoke dope. It's the same feeling you get from accomplishing a goal. Me? I smoke meth and feel like I'm back in law school."

Bird blinks. "I don't get it."

"What's to get?" I tell him. "I quit."

Bird looks over the field again. There's nothing out there. A frozen pond. Empty sky. At Dick's house, Angie is probably changing leg bandages, unwrapping bloody strips of gauze and setting them aside. Or she's throwing plates against the walls. They're one of those couples. When they were married, Dick and Angie would down fifths of whiskey and gin and would start fights in rotation, in whoever-was-drunker shifts. But the divorce was easy; neither one of them had anything. Which meant they didn't have a thing to lose.

On the other hand, Angie's being back in Dick's life is not necessarily a good thing. The night of the crash, Dick slammed a pint of whiskey and left a note at whatever place Angie was staying at the time, maybe some biker's trailer she'd met down at the Bridge. I don't know. But I know the note. She brought it to the office while I was trying to bill some clients. An oil smudged napkin that read in red pen, "Angie, darlin, if you're reading this, I'm not alive. I wish I could bring you with me."

I think worry or guilt is what ultimately brought Angie back into Dick's life. Or Dick promised her some of the settlement cash. It's not my deal. My deal is the case and whatever makes my job easier. And right now, that's Angie. She's the one who rolls Dick's bloated morphine body out of bed each morning. Without her, Dick neglects. He goes feral. He won't shave or shower or show up to any of his court hearings. He'll sit at home all day, draping bloody strips of gauze over his tub like they were dirty pairs of socks.

"Let's go run Dick up," Bird says.

"He needs rest," I say, feeling like Bird can read my mind. "Besides, there's Angie."

"Nah," Bird says. "She'll be out."

The way Bird talks makes me think he knows something, that maybe Angie's sleeping around.

"They on the rocks?" I ask.

Bird shrugs. A bad omen.

"I may have seen her at the Bridge."

"Seen?"

"Yah."

I look at the clock.

There's still a few more hours until last call. I'd rather not go to Dick's and catch Angie. When Angie's drunk, she can yell a rat out of a sack of dog food, but I need to talk to Dick before the filing deadline, translate some of his suffering into legalese. Besides, I should check in on him. It's been awhile.

Either way, Bird doesn't care about the case, or even Dick for that matter. He's after the codeine and whatever else is treating Dick's phantom pain.

"Come on," Bird says. "Besides, I bet Dick's got something for us to get into."

Bird takes the backroads to Dick's house. Even if he was sober, Bird shouldn't be on the roads. He got slapped with a restricted last year, but that doesn't keep him from getting around. I stopped the court from installing a breathalyzer on his starter, which makes me too skilled an attorney for my brother's own good.

The Chevy Silverado we're driving around in is nearly rusted through to the floorboards. Bird got it from some junker out in Bloomingdale. Besides the frame, the power steering doesn't work, except to turn right, and the four wheel drive is bunk. A pile of loose cinder blocks sliding across the bed is the only thing keeping the truck from slipping on the ice. It's too dangerous a rig for me to get around in, but just dangerous enough for my brother Bird.

"Dick's got problems," Bird says over the loud exhaust. "I fix my problems. You know why?"

Bird's sitting behind the wheel, leaning on the armrest. It's too short a drive, too long a life, but I take the bait anyway.

"I fix your problems," I say.

"Not my point," Bird says. "I wouldn't do what he did to somebody. It's the worst thing you can do."

"It's his choice," I say.

"That's how you see it," Bird says.

"He's got Angie," I say.

Bird shifts in the driver's seat. "I've thought about it before," he says. "But I would never do it."

I sit there and let the comment go cold between us. I don't know what Bird's capable of, but I take him at his word. Up ahead, headlights gleam over a hill. The roads are all ice and snow and I'm worried Bird won't remember to dim his lights as the other car crests.

"Your brights," I say.

"Compassion," Bird says. "That's what Dick needs."

Bird is still digging around his shirt pocket for a cigarette and the other car's headlights sharpen on the horizon.

"Your brights," I say again.

Bird squints at the oncoming traffic and I notice the truck's broken steering has drifted us left, toward the medium. The other car is just a moment away and I can already feel the head-on collision, the shock of the frame as it folds in on us like a bellows.

"Bird!" I yell, making a move towards the windshield.

In a single motion, Bird jerks the truck back to the right side of the road and flips off his brights. The other car mounts the hill and passes by with plenty of space. The cigarette in Bird's pocket is now pinned between his fingers and he goes to light it.

"When'd you get so jumpy?" he asks.

At Dick's, I expect Angie to answer the door, but she doesn't. Dick greets us from his wheelchair. He's wearing a flannel shirt and pajama bottoms, which are decorated with little snowmen and green elves. He tells us to get in and shut the door already.

Inside, I look around for signs of Angie.

There are none. A smell like dead mice is seeping out of the trash and wafting into the kitchen. In the sink, a week-old T-bone steak has fused to a ratty dish towel. The counters are covered in moldy potato peels, chewed-up corn cobs and miscellaneous trash.

"You composting?" Bird asks.

Dick ignores the comment and wheels himself into the living room, next to the couch. He sits there and rubs his thighs. His legs are wrapped in bandages the color of salmon.

"Angie out buying groceries or something?" I ask.

"Went out," Dick says.

Bird pulls out three tiny bottles of liquor from his coat pocket.

"Let her go," Bird says. He offers Dick a tiny bottle of whiskey.

"I'm sober," Dick says.

Bird shrugs. He twists the tiny cap off and drinks the shot himself.

"How are you feeling?" I ask. "About your surgery?"

"How do you think I'm feeling?"

I look down at my feet, try to imagine it. If my legs were stumps, I'd probably have to cast my body down to the floor just to get out of here. I'd have to scoot across the piss-stained carpet on my ass. I look back at the kitchen. Cigarette butts and pop bottles breach the trash can's horizon. Dick notices me notice the mess.

"Haven't tidied up," he says.

"Sure," I say. "Must be difficult."

"Difficult?" Bird holds the nubs of his ring and pinky fingers up for everyone to see, the fingers he cut off two years ago with a circular saw. "It's emotional. Feels worse than getting cheated on."

Dick looks up. "What," he says. "You used to walk on those?"

"Worse than that." Bird drops a cigarette into an empty beer can. "Used to get myself off. And sometimes a lady. Now, I don't have that kind of grip."

Dick half-chuckles and rolls his chair over to the coffee table. There's a game of Monopoly spread across the surface with pieces still on it.

"It's kind of like that," Dick says.

I pick up a green monopoly house and think about a person's ability to walk. The value of it. Dick wants at least eight hundred thousand dollars. I'd let mine go for less.

"Where'd Angie crawl to?" Bird asks.

"It's been hard on her," Dick says.

"Her?" Bird wrings the word dry of resentment. *"She's* having a hard time?"

Dick doesn't respond. A silence builds between us. Dick rolls himself over to the coffee table and picks up loose Monopoly hotels and dollar bills and sets them aside. He pushes away ashtrays and empty beer cans until he's unearthed a clean stretch of table for Bird to snort pills off of. On the television, Niles Crane from *Frasier* lights up a fat cigar. He's dressed in a tuxedo.

"Rich boy," Bird says. He points at the TV. "You gonna start wearing one of those?"

Dick tosses a little orange bottle of pills over to Bird and Bird's got three lines ready to go in no time. He snorts one with rolled up Monopoly money and then holds the money out for me. My line goes down smooth and easy and soon my head feels like someone's standing tall inside it, pushing up on the ceiling.

"Rich boy," Dick says. "I like it."

"You'd look fat in a tux," Bird says.

"I am fat," says Dick.

Bird snorts up the last line of pills and we all watch the TV again. The characters are all walking around a sky rise apartment and I'm surprised at the furniture and hardwood floors and all the nice things they got crammed in there, the mountain on the horizon.

"I want one of those," Dick says.

"One of what?" I ask.

"A dog."

A small terrier jumps into an old man's lap on the screen. It sits obediently as the old man pets it.

"Just a little guy," Dick says. "Something to keep up with."

"Shit, we can get you a dog," Bird says. "How about we do something? Go shooting?"

"I don't feel like killing," Dick says.

"Killing?" Bird sounds offended. "Who said anything about killing?"

Dick shrugs. "Not up for it."

"I'd like to hike a mountain," I say. And then I remember about Dick's legs and I feel embarrassed for even saying it. "See a mountain, I mean."

Dick rubs his balding head. "I never liked to hike. Maybe I missed out."

Bird turns, wild-eyed, and I can tell right away the drugs have dropped in his throat. "What's stopping you?" Bird asks.

"That a joke?" says Dick.

There's a pause between commercials. A build-up.

"No joke," Bird says. "You're cooped up in here because you want to be. Remember David Rhodes? Remember his three legged

Rottweiler-mutt? That dog ran after everything. It'd jump at the chance to hike a mountain."

Dick finds the mute button on the remote, squares Bird up in his chair.

"You comparing me to a dog?" he says.

Bird sips his beer. "I just want you to feel better is all. Want you to remember you're still living. And I'm glad for it. That's called compassion."

Dick looks down at the Monopoly box. The show cuts back to life.

"She wishes I died," Dick says.

I look away at the TV, at anything besides Dick.

"She wishes the accident killed me," Dick goes on. "She said that. Just today. Talk about compassion. You think I'm going to give her a piece of my settlement?"

Bird stands up, tosses another one of his little liquor bottles at Dick's chair. Dick doesn't catch it.

"Now you're talking," Bird says. "That's why we're here. Baby boy wanted to talk to you about your case."

"Then talk," Dick says.

Dick changes the angle of his chair so it faces the TV again. He's turned away from me. Now's a bad time to remind him that he was at-fault for the collision. Forget about Angie. There's the blood tests to worry about. He should be in prison right now, not filing lawsuits. But tonight's not the time to say it.

"I can see you're not up for it," I say.

Dick looks at me.

"Don't give me that. You're here," he says. "Go ahead."

"Well," I say. "This is a hard case. If it goes to trial, and it's looking that way, then I need to work the right angles. I need to hear how you'd tell it."

"Tell what?" Dick asks.

I point to Dick's chair, his legs.

"What it means. You know, *your situation*."

Dick looks at me for a minute, but then something on the TV catches his attention. He turns toward the screen.

"They say I can do anything I used to," he says. "The rehab people even explained to me how my dick works, because you know what? It still does. But Angie's too scared to touch it. And that's how it is. Understand? Everything's different, but I haven't changed a bit. It's like you two right now, trying to roll my ass up a mountain."

Dick's being sincere. He goes on. "The doctors said I had a one in a million shot to even survive. They think my life is a lotto ticket. Imagine this on a scratch off."

Bird sits up on the sofa, interrupts. "That's the kind of shit I'm talking about. A dog doesn't care about things like that. A dog just lives its life."

"I ain't a dog," Dick says.

A few moments go by. I don't say anything else and neither does Bird. The show cuts to another commercial break, but we're all watching like it's the climax, like it's going to tell us something important about ourselves. I'm thinking about leaving, about how to go about it, when Bird gets up and abruptly walks out of the room. A few seconds later, his truck roars to life outside and he comes stomping back in, right up behind Dick, pushing at the back of his wheelchair.

"What the hell are you doing?" Dick asks.

"You're driving," Bird says. "I'm shooting. Baby boy, you're gonna spot in the back."

Dick's trying to pull the handbrake down on his wheelchair, but Bird tugs his fingers up, pushes Dick's chair out into the driveway, next to the truck. I get out there and look around and see what Bird's got rigged up. He zip-tied a hand claw, which the courts gave him for picking up trash, to the gas pedal. It's a hillbilly hand accelerator and when Dick sees it he frowns.

"There ain't no brakes," Dick says.

"Don't need brakes," says Bird. "All it needs is a sober driver."

Dick thinks it over a minute and does something I don't expect. He goes along. "Lift me up," he says.

Bird and I grab the fat of Dick's ass and lift him out of his chair. We put him behind the wheel, tuck his wheelchair away in the space between the front and backseats. I pile in and watch Dick get good and comfortable in the driver's seat. It's the first time he's driven since the accident, maybe the last time because of the way the case is going. It's not like Dick is going to keep his license.

"What's that?" Dick asks. He's looking at Bird's rifle.

"A .22," Bird says.

"You hunting squirrel with that?"

"We're just shooting," Bird says. "Drive us out of here."

Dick swings the truck into drive and taps gently down on the hand claw. The truck lurches forward, spazzes down the driveway.

"There you go," Bird says. "Nice and easy. Get on the light."

I hit the spotlight and spread the beam down either side of the driveway. It's a long driveway, about a half-mile, with corn fields to either side. We don't see any deer, or raccoons or anything else to shoot. I expect Dick to pull a uey at the end of the road, but he doesn't. Instead, he takes us down 108th, towards Pullman, and speeds up a little. I cut the spotlight off and put my palms down on the backseat beside me.

"There you go," Bird says. "Ain't lost a step. Driving straight as ever."

Dick's looking ahead at the road, ignoring us. One of his hands is resting on the steering wheel while the other applies an even pressure to the hand claw. We're speeding up from twenty miles per hour, to thirty, and soon we're pushing thirty five. I imagine driving has got to feel good to Dick. Like getting a piece of his life back. Like finding something lost.

"You're zooming," I tell him.

"That's right," Bird adds. "So you can cut that hiking horseshit."

Dick doesn't say anything. He applies a little more pressure to the accelerator. He takes us up to forty miles per hour, then forty five. I'm sitting in the backseat rubbing my palms against the fabric of my jeans, pinching the seams of my pants, bouncing my legs up and down, feeling the tendons behind my knees, my calf muscling bulging, going slack. For the first time in my life, I'm actually *feeling* my legs. And I want to say something. Something about the case, about life, about Dick getting his mind right, but I don't have time to. The shape of a deer appears in our headlights. It's stumbling up ahead of us near the shoulder, looking sick or hurt, from what, I can't tell.

"Brake!" Bird shouts.

I think maybe it's too slick to stop, but I don't have time to say it because everything happens so fast. Dick presses down on the hand claw as hard as he can and then jerks the wheel, squares the doe up in his headlights and spears it at fifty-plus miles per hour. The deer goes bouncing up over the grill, over the windshield, and the bricks in the back slam up on one side of the bed, sending the truck into a spin across the road. Out of control, we swing into the ditch and I have just enough time to crouch down and hold the back of my head while the bricks in the back come crashing into the cab, shattering glass, clunking off the backs of our seats.

And then it's all over.

I look up and see the windshield splintered into a spider's web. The headlights beam face down into a snowbank like a flashlight held to the palm of your hand. I wiggle my feet and feel the bricks on the floor of the cab. There's glass all around me. It's cutting into my arms and legs and I cough on the fine glass floating in the air. Sound comes screaming back into my life and I realize it's Bird. He's yelling about his truck.

"Fucking crash my shit!" Bird tries punching his way out the passenger door. "Stupid, crazy, fuck!"

I feel Bird's body heave in the front seat, shaking the truck's wrecked hull. He can't get out because the frame snapped and is pinning the doors closed. I take a deep breath and close my eyes and when I open them, I see Dick's bloody face in the rearview mirror. He's brushing glass off the ends of his shirt sleeves and using them to wipe the blood from his eyes. The only thing I can think to do is sit there and wait for a moment, for the pain or for something else, I don't know.

"Seatbelts," Dick says. He shakes his head. "I'm sorry."

The truck goes quiet except for an annoying dashboard beep. I should be worried about Dick and Bird, but I'm worried about cops, about blood alcohol content and repeat offenses and all the trouble we need to beat. I'm worrying so hard I almost don't notice Dick whimpering in front of me. He's leaning over the steering wheel now, heaving like a child.

"You hurt?" I ask.

Dick shakes his head. "I'm fucked."

Bird has calmed down a little and is watching Dick closely. He makes a fist as if to punch him, but instead, he grabs the back of Dick's neck, squeezes gently. "You owe me a new one. Something better when baby boy wins your case. I'm not playing."

I stumble over myself. I don't know what to say so I lie. "This case, you know. It's a life changer."

The truck goes quiet. A breeze blows snow in the cab. We need to leave. Bird and I climb out the broken windows, bust the door free and get Dick back in his wheelchair. I remember to sling the .22 over my shoulder and pocket the flashlight. Bird has already chucked the empty beer bottles into the woods.

We start down the road, but Dick is stuck in place. His wheels are bent on their axles and we find his chair impossible to push. I ask Dick if he's alright to be carried back home, but Dick still can't look me in the eyes. Bird and I lift him on our shoulders anyway and limp toward the house.

Up ahead, we see the dim glow of a street lamp, a brown lump moving just underneath it. We walk up there and each turn our heads, see it's a doe. She's laid out in the lamplight, shaking on the shoulder of the road. The littlest speck of fur is disturbed on her forehead and there's something catching the light just above her eyes. It's a bullet. It's lodged smack-dab in the middle of her skull and I realize we must be looking at the doe Bird shot earlier. The doe that Dick just hit.

"Look at that!" Bird yells. He sees it too. "You couldn't kill that deer if you tried!"

The doe's still alive, somehow. She's trying to rise, but her hips are obviously broken. We're standing in front of her like a three-headed, four-legged monster, Dick in the middle, Bird and me on either side.

"That deer should be a splat in the road," Bird says. "Baby boy, why don't you put her down?"

"It might take a couple," I say.

I go to unshoulder the .22 from my free arm, but Dick stops me.

"Be still," he says. "Don't spook her."

I try to be still, to keep from spooking the doe, to keep her from crawling off into the woods, but she's so far gone, so close to death, that it doesn't even matter. It's as if we aren't even there.

Histories My Brothers Taught Me

1. You were hatched like a bird.
2. The yard is a Confederate graveyard.
3. Peter ran away.
4. Mom used to be tan, like a sunflower, like a stick of butter.
5. Pregnancy frazzled her up.
6. You were a mistake. An accident.
7. We had it harder than you.
8. The old house was bigger, filled with walls. It burned down when we were visiting Aunt Paula down in Charleston. Bear, Charlie, and Smoke all died in the fire. We found their bodies charred in our kitchen.
9. Dad and Mom used to go out for dinner. They'd come home happy and drunk.
10. Dad said this house would have a pool.
11. We used to sail Lake Michigan. Dad owned boats the size of states and we'd float out every fourth of July.
12. The adults stayed topside and we sat below deck, trading cards and stealing drinks of rum. One time, Sammy got plastered and threw up on the walls. Mom said, "Oh Sam, dear, you're seasick."
13. When Dad says, "I've spent too many days in the Navy," he means: "Nobody wants to see your mother in a bathing suit."

14. In Michigan, the winters are brutal.
15. Our neighbor, Big John, used to plow our driveway. He'd show after every big storm. We dug caves in the piles of snow.
16. One day, Dad and Mom both got stuck in our driveway and Dad walked over to give Big John hell. Apparently, Big John had shot himself. He'd been lying around his house dead for weeks. That night, Dad got drunk and told us about it.
17. He said, "Some things people just weren't meant to see."
18. Dad used to say work was easy. He used to sell houses and buy out companies. We used to be rich, you know?
19. Mom used to work before she had you. She was a hygienist and cleaned people's teeth.
20. "Teeth say a lot about a person," she used to say. She made us brush three times a day, made it our duty to floss.
21. Mom was a general at war with cavities, with junk food and all things unsafe.
22. When Sammy broke his arm on the diving board, he told everyone he'd dodged a train. Mrs. Stein pulled Mom aside at parent teacher conferences and recommended Sammy see a counselor. She said, "Karen, I'm sorry, but it's a lot for a boy."
23. Dad used to have people over. They'd stay up all night and keep us awake. Sometimes, Mom would throw parties. She'd make costumes and was always dressed in this or that. We always had something to do.
24. Peter was our sidekick. We called him Little Pete. Stinky Pete. Peter Cottontail.
25. Peter liked to play basketball, more than even you. Dad put together a little hoop for him in our driveway. He set up cones and painted lines, gave Peter a place to dribble, another to shoot.
26. Peter died instantly.
27. Sammy found the spot where his head exploded in the driveway. A brown and faded stain on the concrete. Sammy

chalked it off like one of those investigators you see on TV. There was so much blood, you would have puked.

28. Mom quit her job and put together puzzles. We'd help her sort pieces by color and shape. Sometimes, she'd lean back and pet our heads. She'd smile and say thank you. Other times, she left the room.
29. On Christmas, we got her a ten thousand piece. A big old puzzle of a man and a river and a canoe. She put it together in one afternoon, had it framed by New Year's Eve.
30. We played Pillowball. The puzzle marked the end zone—the spot you passed to score points. You could play Pillowball one-on-one, or three-on-three, but it had to be odd. Sammy played unfair. He'd climb the furniture and rile up our dogs. He'd run behind them, use their bodies to block. It was a rough sport and Sammy was ruthless. He was Mr. Pillowball. Pillow Bowl MVP.
31. You would've never made it.
32. One day, Sammy tackled our friend into the wall and broke mom's puzzle. We stood around like we'd killed someone, like we'd shot that old man and stole his empty canoe. Dad swept up the pieces and tossed them out.
33. "It's all a waste of time," he said.
34. Mom never went back to work, not even when Dad lost the business. She took to sleeping and eating all day.
35. You can tell a creditor by the pause on the phone. Dad told us never to answer, but we knew how to play it smooth.
36. "Wrong number," we'd say.
37. Dad used to say money was pretend.
38. "I'm bankrupt, not broke," he'd tell us.
39. We moved down South because it was cheap.
40. "Prudent," Dad said.
41. The heat was less bad up in Michigan. You could play outside all day and nothing ever dried up.

42. The old house sold cheap because of the fire. It was nothing, just a little smoke. We packed away everything and Dad gave up our dogs. There were so many boxes—so much space we could've used.
43. Dad gave Peter's stuff to Goodwill.
44. "To folks that might need it," he said.
45. Mom dragged boxes out of Peter's room. They were full of rink-dink T-shirts and stuffed animals, X-Men comics and other things Peter liked to pick through. Cyclops was Peter's favorite hero. He shot lasers from his eyes. He would blink and chase us around. "Zap! Zap!" he'd yell. And then: "You're dead!"
46. Dad's truck backed right over Peter. Killed Peter with his car.
47. Sammy saw it.
48. Dad yelled like a rocket, jerked Sammy away by the arm.
49. "Do *not* come out here," he told us.
50. We stood tiptoe at the window and saw brake lights, a blue sky, poofy clouds.
51. Sammy coached Peter at basketball. He'd have him shoot free throws and run drills. He kept Peter out later than he was supposed to. The basketballs you have come from Peter. Your hoop used to be in Peter's room.
52. When Mom hauled out the last of Peter's boxes, she laid on the carpet and cried. Dad hugged her like you would a dog, like a sick person squirming in bed. "You killed my son," she said.
53. Dad cupped his hands over Mom's mouth and pushed down like he was giving her jaw CPR. She squirmed and shivered and globs of her snot slimed down the back of Dad's hands. Dad drove his palm down into her nose.
54. We watched them and didn't do a thing. What do you think we could even do?
55. The drive down here took two whole days. We lived off Cheetos and chips.

56. Dad got a good job when the markets straightened out, when people started spending money and buying houses again.
57. Mom got pregnant and ate herself fat.
58. We collected detentions like tickets at the arcade and were sons at the foot of a bed.
59. We had it harder than you.
60. Looking out, Lake Michigan is as big as the Atlantic. You would never believe it's a lake.

Acknowledgements

I would like to thank the editors and literary journals that have published previous versions of the following stories: "Ed's Baby" was originally published in *Bat City Review* no. 14 (2018); "Histories My Brothers Taught Me" appeared in *Bridge Eight Press Online* (2018).

I would like to thank my parents, Jim and Erin, for their love and support. My brother, Justin, and sister, Dana, for their companionship. My grandfathers, Paul Shek and Robert Wood, for the stories they have lived and told.

I would like to thank all of my teachers at Western Michigan University and the University of Alaska Fairbanks. I'm especially grateful to Sue Ellen Christian, Daryl Farmer, Thisbe Nissen, Kyle Mellen, Sara Johnson, Dan Mancilla, Gerri Brightwell, Richard Katrovas and Noah Hilgert. Without their teaching this book wouldn't be possible.

I would also like to thank my cohort at the University of Alaska Fairbanks for the long hours and dark winter nights spent workshopping and discussing these stories. Rich Carr, the English Department Chair at UAF, as well as the graduate college, for awarding me a teaching assistantship. Ed Finnerty, Mickey Ciokajlo, Danielle Salisbury, Rex Hall and all my colleagues at the Kalamazoo Gazette and Jackson Citizen Patriot for helping me navigate the world of journalism.

A thanks is due to the close friends I have known throughout the years, Aaron Ainsworth, Gage Waanders, Josh Gilley, Tom Jacobs, Steve Sewell and Andrew Schafer.

I would also like to thank Hadley Moore, Kevin Avery and the entire staff at Michigan Writers for their willingness to put this work into the world.

Finally, I would like to thank Samara Taber for her love, trust and acceptance.

About the Judge

Michigan Writers Cooperative Press would like to express our thanks to HADLEY MOORE for judging the fiction manuscripts in our chapbook contest this year. We are grateful for her commitment of time, energy, and expertise to all of the contestants' manuscripts. Thank you, Hadley, for helping Michigan Writers Cooperative Press develop and publish this new literary voice.

Hadley Moore's collection *Not Dead Yet and Other Stories* won Autumn House Press's 2018 fiction contest and is out now. Her short stories, novel excerpts, and nonfiction have appeared widely in many publications, including *Newsweek, McSweeney's Quarterly Concern, Witness, Alaska Quarterly Review, Indiana Review, Anomaly* (formerly *Drunken Boat*), *The Drum, Sequestrum, Midwestern Gothic,* and other publications. She is at work on a novel and another story collection, and is an alum of the MFA Program for Writers at Warren Wilson College.

Not Dead Yet studies the uncertainties of loss, turning a gaze toward the often-silenced voices of the infirm, elderly, and adolescent. Rich in humor and honesty, Moore's debut collection of short stories dives into moments of absurdity and tragedy by presenting a contemporary set of narratives from a lush cast of characters who are coping with the voids left by the passing of youth, happiness, and fulfillment.

About the Author

Ryan Shek is a writer from Southwest Michigan. A graduate of Western Michigan University's journalism program, Ryan has worked as a crime reporter for the *Kalamazoo Gazette* and *Jackson Citizen Patriot*. His journalism has won Michigan AP awards for feature writing and spot news coverage. In 2020, Ryan earned his MFA in fiction from the University of Alaska Fairbanks where he now teaches English composition. His short stories have appeared in *Bridge Eight Press, Bat City Review,* and *Stonecrop Magazine.*

About Michigan Writers Cooperative Press

This book was published in the spring of 2021 in a signed edition of 100 copies.

This chapbook is part of the Cooperative Series of the Michigan Writers Small Press Project, which was launched in 2005 to give members of Michigan Writers, Inc. a new avenue to publication. All of the chapbooks in this series are an author's first book in that genre. The Cooperative Press shoulders the publishing costs for the first edition, and writers share the marketing and promotional responsibilities in return for the prestige of being published by a press that prints only carefully selected manuscripts.

Chapbook length manuscripts of poetry, short stories, and essays are solicited each year from members and adjudicated by a panel of experienced writers and a judge who is a specialist in a particular genre. For more information, please visit www.michwriters.org.

MICHIGAN WRITERS is an open-membership organization dedicated to providing opportunities for networking, professional growth, and publication for writers of all ages and skill levels in Northwest Michigan and beyond.

MANAGING EDITOR: Liam Strong, Kevin Avery

READERS: Kevin Avery, Susan Odgers, Patricia Trentacoste, Sarah Wangler

BOOK DESIGN: Amy Hansen, Daniel Stewart

Other Titles Available
from Michigan Writers Cooperative Press

The Grace of the Eye by Michael Callaghan
Trouble With Faces by Trinna Frever
Box of Echoes by Todd Mercer
Beyond the Reach of Imagination by Duncan Spratt Moran
The Grass Impossibly by Holly Wren Spaulding
The Chocolatier Speaks of his Wife by Catherine Turnbull
Dangerous Exuberance by Leigh Fairey
Point of Sand by Jaimien Delp
Hard Winter, First Thaw by Jenny Robertson
Friday Nights the Whole Town Goes to the Basketball Game by Teresa J. Scollon
Seasons for Growing by Sarah Baughman
Forking the Swift by Jennifer Sperry Steinorth
The Rest of Us by John Mauk
Kisses for Laura by Joan Schmeichel
Eat the Apple by Denise Baker
First Risings by Michael Hughes
Fathers and Sons by Bruce L. Makie
Exit Wounds by Jim Crockett
The Solid Living World by Ellen Stone
Bitter Dagaa by Robb Astor
Crime Story by Kris Kuntz
Michaela by Gabriella Burman
Supposing She Dreamed This by Gail Wallace Bozzano
Line and Hook by Kevin Griffin
And Sarah His Wife by Christina Diane Campbell
Proud Flesh by Nancy Parshall
Angel Rides a Bike by Margaret Fedder
Ink by Kathleen Pfeiffer
What Will You Teach Her? by Megan Klco Kellner
The Mountain Ash by Kathleen Rabbers

Michigan
WRITERS

www.ingramcontent.com/pod-product-compliance
Lightning Source LLC
Chambersburg PA
CBHW021745190726
48288CB00009B/3167

* 9 7 8 1 9 5 0 7 4 4 0 4 6 *